For Jack and Betty, and my sisters who shared my peculiar pets
—V xx

For Lola and Cordelia
—love D

tiger tales
an imprint of ME Media, LLC
202 Old Ridgefield Road, Wilton, CT 06897
Published in the United States 2010
Originally published in Great Britain 2009
by Alison Green Books
an imprint of Scholastic Children's Books
Text copyright © 2009 Victoria Roberts
Illustrations copyright © 2009 Deborah Allwright
CIP data is available
ISBN-13: 978-1-58925-089-5
ISBN-10: 1-58925-089-3
Printed in Singapore
TWP0709
1 3 5 7 9 10 8 6 4 2

by Victoria Roberts

Illustrated by
Deborah Allwright

The Best Pet Ever

tiger tales

Mom, can I have a pet?
Please?
Mom, Mom, can I?
Can I have a pet?

We'll see.

So I see. . . .
I see a rock. A smooth rock.
I tie a string around it.

I call him **Fluffy.**

I take Fluffy for walks.

I let him off his leash
if he's good.

And he's good . . . for a day or two.

Mom, can I have a pet? Please?
Mom, Mom, can I?
Can I have a pet?

We'll see.

So I see....
I see a glove.
A soft, woolly glove.

I put her in a basket.
I call her **Nibbles**.

I tickle Nibbles
in her basket.

I feed her
when she's hungry.

And she's hungry...

for a day or two.

Mom, can I have a pet?
Please?
Mom, Mom, can I?
Can I have a pet?

We'll see.

So I see....

I see a candy wrapper.
A shiny candy wrapper.

I put it in a bowl.
I call him **Swishy**.

I give Swishy water.
   I see him twist and turn as he swims.

And he swims . . .

for a day or two.

Mom, can I have a pet? **Please?**
Mom, Mom, can I?
Can I have a pet?

We'll see.

So I see....
   I see a balloon.
      A round balloon.

I draw a face on it.
   I call him BRUCE.

I pet Bruce.

And he sticks to me when we hug.

And we hug . . .

and we play . . .

and we dance around. . . .
And Bruce is the best pet ever . . .

for a day or two.

N G!

Mom, Mom!

My pet popped!

He was the best pet ever
and now I can't play with him.

Oh, that's a shame.
Don't worry.
Maybe we can find another
pet for you to play with.

Let's see....

So we see....

We see a box.
A cardboard box.
We lift the lid.
We peek inside.

And we see...

Timmy the kitten!

And Timmy is the best pet

in the world!